Olive, THE other REINDEER.

Vivian Walsh and J. otto Seibold

illustrated by J. otto Seibold

chronicle books · san francisco

Sophie
Merry
Christmas
2007
yo yo

dedicated to.

anna
O'ROURKE

This deluxe edition published in 2007 by Chronicle Books LLC.

Book design by J.otto Seibold.
Paper engineering by Ray Marshall.
Typeset in Palentino and Nico.
The illustrations in this book were digitally rendered.
Manufactured in China.

Library of Congress Cataloging-in-Publication Data
Seibold, J.otto.
Olive, the other reindeer / by J.otto Seibold and Vivian Walsh. — 1st deluxe ed.
p. cm.
Summary: Thinking that "all of the other reindeer" she hears people singing about include her,
Olive the dog reports to the North Pole to help Santa Claus on Christmas Eve. Includes lift-up
flaps, scratch-and-sniff panels, and a pop-up.
ISBN-13: 978-0-8118-5719-2
ISBN-10: 0-8118-5719-0
1. Toy and movable books—Specimens. [1. Reindeer—Fiction. 2. Dogs—Fiction. 3. Christmas—
Fiction. 4. Santa Claus—Fiction. 5. Toy and movable books.] I. Seibold, J.otto, ill. II. Title.
PZ7.S45513Ol 2007
[Fic]—dc22
2006031861

Distributed in Canada by Raincoast Books
9050 Shaughnessy Street, Vancouver, British Columbia V6P 6E5

10 9 8 7 6 5 4 3 2 1

Chronicle Books LLC
680 Second Street, San Francisco, California 94107

www.chroniclekids.com

very day, Olive took her daily dog walk, winter, spring, summer, or fall.
Today was a winter's day. It was the holidays. There was music playing outdoors.

People were singing along,
"All of the other reindeer..."

Olive was too shy to sing.
"Hmmm-hmm-hm-hm-hmmm-hmmm-hmmm,"
she hummed.

Back at her dog house, Olive was wrapping presents and listening to the radio. She heard that same song again.

"All of the other reindeer..." went the song.
"Olive, the other reindeer..." Olive sang along.

"Olive...the Reindeer," said Olive. "I thought I was a dog. Hmmm, I must be a reindeer!"

It was the time of year when all reindeer reported to the North Pole to help Santa Claus.

Olive put down her scissors carefully, and marched out the door.

She took one bus…

…and then two buses.

She got there just in time.

Santa was checking his list for the second time. Elves were busy helping the reindeer and loading the sleigh with presents for all of the good girls and boys. Everyone was getting ready to go.

Olive took her place.

Santa noticed that there was a little dog in the line-up. Santa knew a lot about dogs— for instance, they can't fly. But as it was time to go, he decided to give Olive a chance.

Comet, the biggest reindeer, used a piece of extra ribbon to make sure Olive was tied in safe and tight.

Now they were ready to go.

Olive was surprised it was so easy to fly.

The other reindeer were very curious about the new helper. They looked at Olive so much—they weren't watching where they were going.

CRASH!

They flew smack into the top of a too tall tree!

"Oh dear," said Santa. "My sleigh is stuck in this tree. I'll have to cut it free."

Olive clung to the side of the tree. She tried to fly up to help Santa…but she could not.

She climbed up slowly and started chewing. Chewing sticks was something Olive could do well.

"Thank you, Olive," said Santa Claus, as they got back on their way.

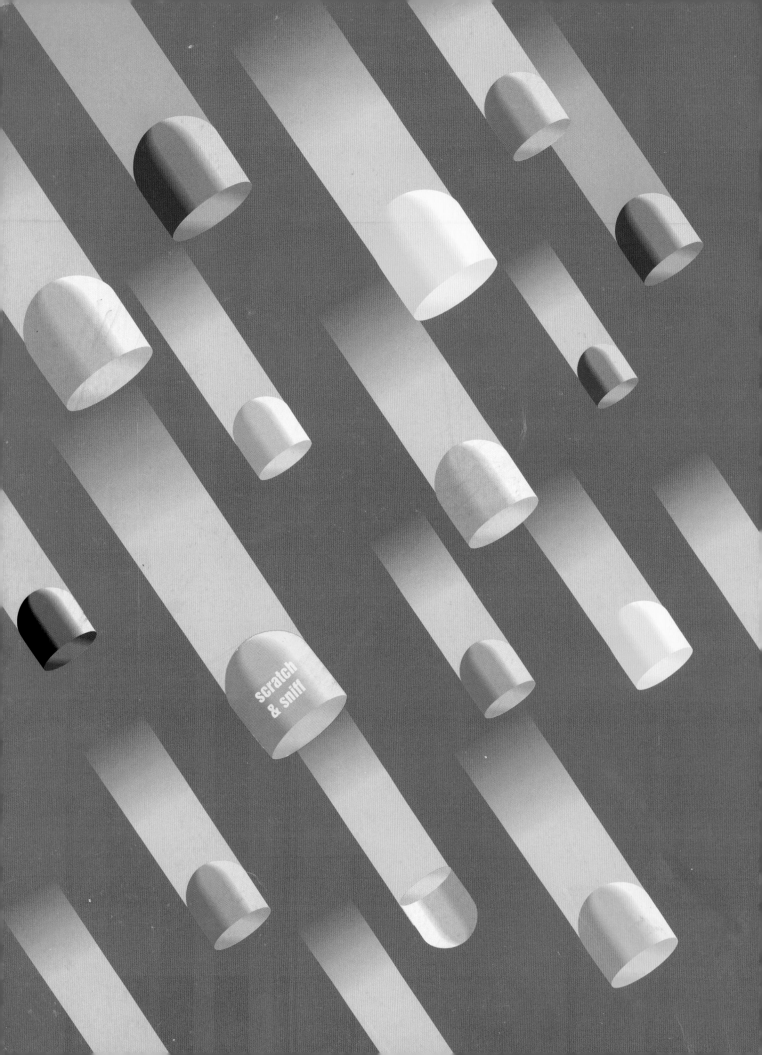

scratch
& sniff

They had not traveled far when Olive's nose began to twitch. Olive smelled trouble. It was the smell of gumdrop candies as they fell from the sleigh.

DROP... DROP... DROP...

Olive barked and Santa knew what to do.

He steered the reindeer down and around so that all of the gumdrops fell,

plop...plop...plop...

back into the toy sack.

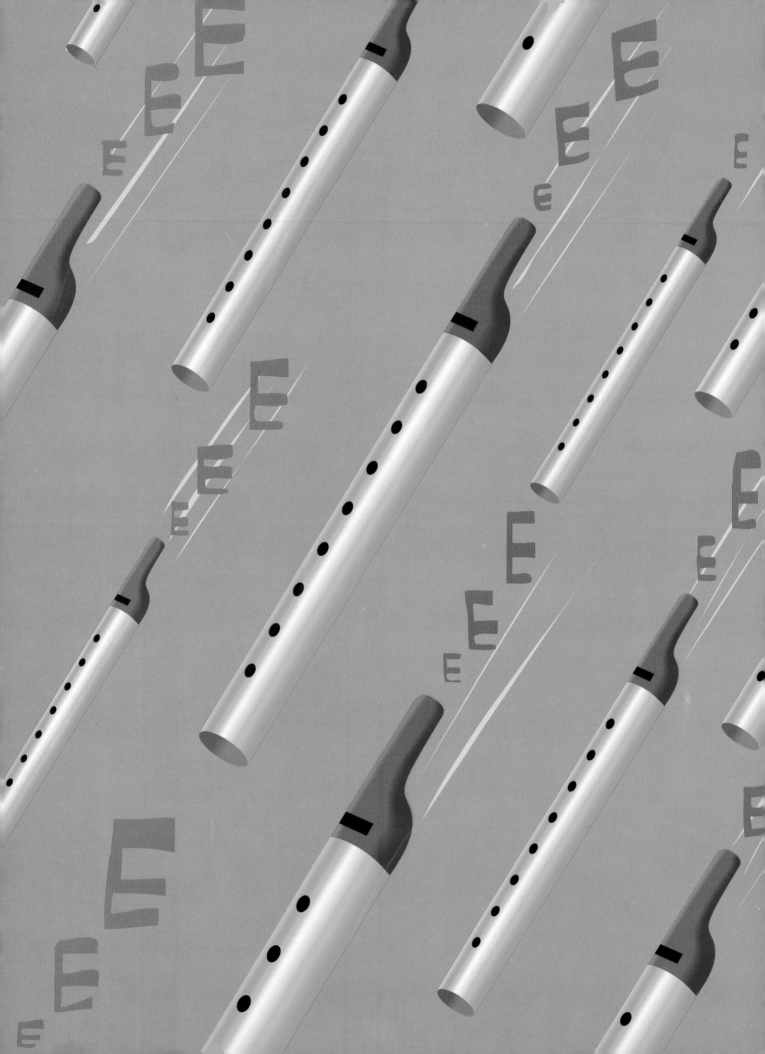

"We were very lucky to not lose a single gumdrop,"
thought Olive. Then she heard a strange sound.
It was the musical note,

EEEEEEEEE.

She spun around on her string to see the night sky
filled with falling flutes.
Olive had to howl louder than the wind instruments.
This was not music to Santa's ears.

"First gumdrops and now flutes," thought Santa.
"That tree must have torn a hole in my sled."

"Prepare for an Emergency Landing,"
Santa instructed.

The sleigh landed in a snowy field full of flutes. Luckily, Olive was very good at fetching sticks. It is something dogs love to do.

Before Santa had finished patching the hole in
the sleigh, Olive had returned each and every
flute back to the sack.

"Ho, ho, ho," said Santa, "we're ready to go."

They were running late. But after a while all the good children…

…received their presents, and Santa and his team headed home.

They were almost home when they got caught in the dreaded North Pole fog. The reindeer slowed down until it was only the breeze that moved them along. The fog was as thick as a pillow. It made everyone feel sleepy.

Then Santa remembered something about dogs—they are expert smellers!

"Olive, I'd hate to be late for breakfast this year," he said. "Mrs. Claus has planned a parade of cookies. Mmmmm, you can almost smell them, can't you?" Olive could smell the cookies.

"Olive, won't you guide my sleigh this morning?" asked Santa.

Olive moved to the front of the reindeer.

scratch & sniff

Back at the North Pole, it was a glorious morning.
After eating lots of good food,
it was time to open presents.

The reindeer got jump ropes and the elves got toy trains.
Santa reached into his toy sack.
There was just one present left.
It was for Olive.
It was her very own set of
reindeer antlers.
They fit perfectly.

Then everyone went outside to play reindeer games.

THE END